For all my family
with love

MADELEINE WINCH

COME BY CHANCE

Crown Publishers, Inc.
New York

Bertha was alone.
She had walked and walked and was far from anywhere.

At the top of the hill she came upon
a tumble-down old house.

She peered in, then she pushed open the door
and crept inside. She could see the house had
been abandoned long ago.

Bertha sat and rested her tired legs,
but her mind wasn't resting at all...

At last she smiled, and set to work.
She mended and patched, swept and scrubbed,
then weeded and watered, until little by little
she had made the house into a cozy home.

She named it "Come by Chance" and nailed up
a sign so everyone would know.
Then, after gathering food and firewood, she settled in.

One cold winter night as Bertha sat by the fire,
a storm began to rage.

The wind whistled and roared,
and the windows rattled and shook.

Dark clouds gathered, then the rain *teemed* down.

Thunder rumbled and lightning flashed through the sky.

"Come by Chance" was the only shelter in sight.

Animals arrived from everywhere!
They were wet, frightened and trembling with cold.
Bertha welcomed them inside and in no time at all
everyone had snuggled up by the warm fire.

As snow began to fall, more and more animals
found their way to the little house on the hill.

"Come by Chance" became so crowded it was almost
bursting, but Bertha left no one out in the cold. Everyone
soon felt at home and night after night they all danced and sang.

Bertha took special care of all her friends,
and together the long winter passed...

After a time,
the sun began to shine and the snow melted.
Flowers blossomed and the hills turned green.
Bertha opened a window.
The air smelled like honey.

It was SPRING!

It was time to part.

"Come again next winter," Bertha called, as one by one
her friends disappeared down the hill.

But Bertha was not alone.
She heard a familiar noise and found
someone had decided to stay.

Now, at the beginning of every winter
there is a great scuffle at the door,
and Bertha and her friend know
that "Come by Chance" will
once again be filled with
music and laughter.

Published in 1990 in the United States
of America by Crown Publishers, Inc.,
a Random House Company.
225 Park Avenue South.
New York, New York 10003.
Printed in Singapore.
Bound in the U.S.A.

Originally published in 1988 in Australia
by Angus & Robertson Publishers.

CROWN is a trademark of Crown Publishers, Inc.

Library of Congress Cataloging-in-Publication Data
Winch, Madeleine. Come by chance.
Summary: When Bertha finds an old tumble-down
house, she turns it into a cozy home and lives
there by herself until the stormy night when
animals come seeking shelter from the rain.
1. Dwellings—Fiction. 2. Animals—Fiction
I. Title.
PZ7.W7219Co 1990   [E]   89-22157
ISBN 0-517-57666-X
ISBN 0-517-57667-8 (lib. bdg.)

10 9 8 7 6 5 4 3 2 1

First American Edition